Dedicated to Marilyn Malin
for putting up with us for so long

Henry Holt and Company, *Publishers since 1866*
Henry Holt® is a registered trademark of Macmillan Publishing Group, LLC
175 Fifth Avenue, New York, New York 10010
mackids.com

ISBN 978-1-62779-867-9
Library of Congress Control Number 2017945035

Our books may be purchased in bulk for promotional, educational, or business use. Please
contact your local bookseller or the Macmillan Corporate and Premium Sales Department at
(800) 221-7945 ext. 5442 or by e-mail at MacmillanSpecialMarkets@macmillan.com.

Originally published in the United Kingdom by Faber & Faber in 2016
First American edition, 2018
Endpaper image used with permission of commentnation.com.
Printed in China by C&C Printing Ltd., Shanghai

1 3 5 7 9 10 8 6 4 2

A Dog Called Bear

diane and christyan fox

GODWINBOOKS

Henry Holt and Company • New York

Lucy had always wanted a dog.
She'd read all the doggy books.
She'd collected doggy pictures from magazines.
She'd saved all her money to buy doggy things.

One day, Lucy set off to find a dog of her own.

Hello. My name is Lucy, and I'm looking for a dog. I have a very nice basket at home, and if I had a dog, I would love him and care for him and take him for walks every day.

But dogs are licky and barky and smelly. I would make a much better pet—as long as I could have a bath every day.

Oh, that's a pity. I only have a shower. Otherwise, I might be very tempted.

Soon Lucy met another animal.

Excuse me. I'm looking for a dog. I have all the food he could eat, and I would love him and care for him and take him for walks every day.

I'm very similar to a dog, but I'm not big on living indoors. Could we try it for three days a week?

Well, I was really looking for a full-time dog. But I can put your name on the list, and if nothing else comes along, I'll let you know.

Excuse me. I'm sorry to bother you,
but I'm a lost dog who's looking for a nice
basket in a home with lots of food, a garden
to play in, and someone to love me and care
for me and take me for walks every day.

What a lucky coincidence!
But are you absolutely sure
you're a dog? I can't find
any like you in my book.

Oh, that must be an old book.
Lots of new dogs have been invented recently.
My name's Bear.

That's a funny name for a dog.
But it is getting late, so I
suppose you'll have to do.

Bear settled in well.
The basket was
a bit small . . .

but the food was
very tasty . . .

the garden was very large . . .

the books were very
informative . . .

the doggy toys
were very fun . . .

and Lucy loved and
cared for him.

But one day, Bear went to sleep.
And he slept through November, December,
January, February, and March.

Which might not have been so bad—
if he hadn't taken all the covers
and all the space in Lucy's bed.

In fact, being a dog owner was more difficult than Lucy had thought.

I can't STAND the mess!

I can't STAND the digging!

I can't STAND the endless bowls of porridge!

Being a pet dog wasn't easy, either.

Well, I'm fed up with having to carry YOUR sticks all the time!

And every time I bring YOUR ball back, YOU throw it away again!

And whenever I try to take a nap, YOU keep waking me up!

One day Bear was so mad, he decided to run away.

But after a day and a night,
Bear missed his basket and his toys.

He missed his garden and he missed the food.
But most of all, he missed Lucy.

Bear realized he was lonely
and had nowhere to go.

A sheet of paper blew
along the ground . . .